Dear Parent:
Your child's love of reading starts here!

Every child learns to read in a different way and at his or her own speed. Some go back and forth between reading levels and read favorite books again and again. Others read through each level in order. You can help your young reader improve and become more confident by encouraging his or her own interests and abilities. From books your child reads with you to the first books he or she reads alone, there are I Can Read Books for every stage of reading:

SHARED READING
Basic language, word repetition, and whimsical illustrations, ideal for sharing with your emergent reader

BEGINNING READING
Short sentences, familiar words, and simple concepts for children eager to read on their own

READING WITH HELP
Engaging stories, longer sentences, and language play for developing readers

READING ALONE
Complex plots, challenging vocabulary, and high-interest topics for the independent reader

ADVANCED READING
Short paragraphs, chapters, and exciting themes for the perfect bridge to chapter books

I Can Read Books have introduced children to the joy of reading since 1957. Featuring award-winning authors and illustrators and a fabulous cast of beloved characters, I Can Read Books set the standard for beginning readers.

A lifetime of discovery begins with the magical words **"I Can Read!"**

Visit www.icanread.com for information
on enriching your child's reading experience.

The

The my little Pony Collection

HARPER

An Imprint of HarperCollinsPublishers

THE MY LITTLE PONY COLLECTION

My Little Pony: Belle of the Ball
Text and illustrations copyright © 2004 Hasbro, Inc.

My Little Pony: Hide-and-Seek
Text and illustrations copyright © 2005 Hasbro, Inc.

My Little Pony: Sleepover Surprise
Text and illustrations copyright © 2006 Hasbro, Inc.

My Little Pony: A Secret Gift
Text and illustrations copyright © 2006 Hasbro, Inc.

My Little Pony: Ponies on Ice
Text and illustrations copyright © 2007 Hasbro, Inc.

My Little Pony: Very Lucky Ponies
Text and illustrations copyright © 2008 Hasbro, Inc.

My Little Pony: Tutus and Toe Shoes
Text and illustrations copyright © 2008 Hasbro, Inc.

My Little Pony: Caps in the Air!
Text and illustrations copyright © 2009 Hasbro, Inc.

ISBN 978-0-06-201214-2

10 11 12 13 14 LEO 10 9 8 7 6 5 4 3 2 1

Go to pages 185–192 to locate the rebuses in the Rebus Chart for each book title. Enjoy!

Table of Contents

I Can Read!™

BEGINNING
1
READING

Belle
of the Ball

by Ruth Benjamin

illustrated by Ken Edwards

HARPER

An Imprint of HarperCollinsPublishers

The  were excited

about the Best Friends' Ball.

Twinkle Twirl was busy

at the dance studio.

Sweetberry was busy

baking a ![cake].

At the ,

the worked hard.

They blew up .

They tied the

with shiny .

Skywishes left the .

She stopped to visit

Twinkle Twirl.

"Do you want to fly a

with me?" asked Skywishes.

"I can't now,"

said Twinkle Twirl.

"I am teaching the

a new dance."

"I will leave the 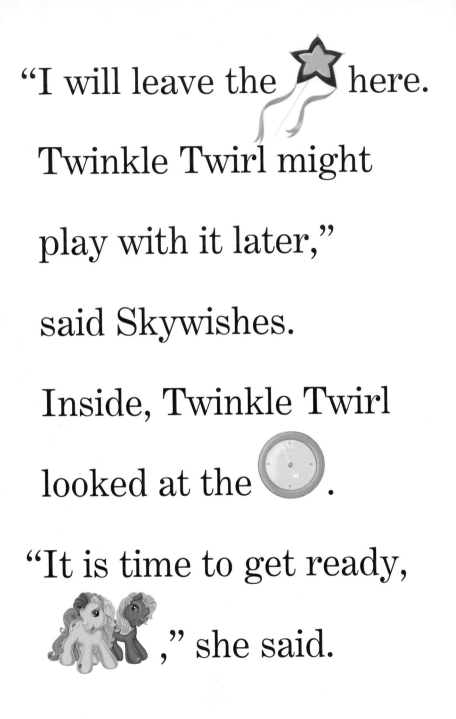 here.

Twinkle Twirl might

play with it later,"

said Skywishes.

Inside, Twinkle Twirl

looked at the .

"It is time to get ready,

," she said.

"May I wear your 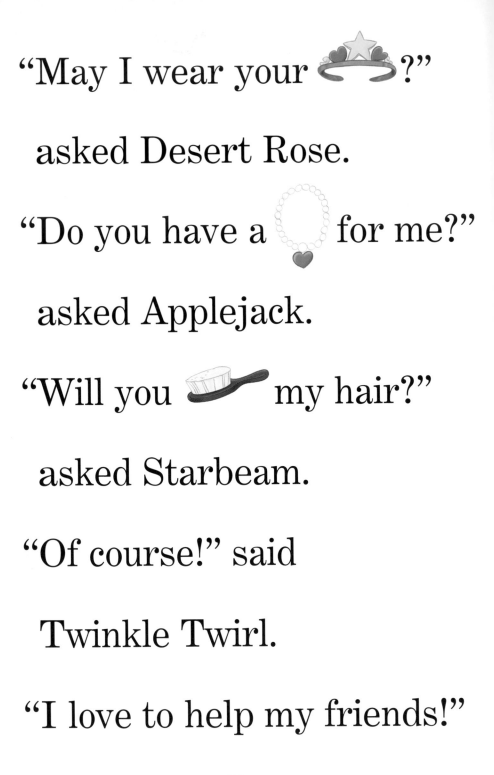?"

asked Desert Rose.

"Do you have a ⬤ for me?"

asked Applejack.

"Will you 🪥 my hair?"

asked Starbeam.

"Of course!" said

Twinkle Twirl.

"I love to help my friends!"

It was time for

Twinkle Twirl to get ready.

She had no .

She had no .

She had no one to

her hair.

How could she go

to the ball?

You're Invited
to the
Best Friend's
Ball!

Twinkle Twirl looked up

at the ⭐⭐.

Skywishes' ⭐ was

flying in the ☁.

"A wishing star!" she said.

"I wish I had a 👑

and a 📿.

Then I could go to the ball."

"Your wishes *will* come true," said a pretty .

 were all around her.

"My name is ⭐ Catcher."

"Wow!" said Twinkle Twirl.

"You are a real pegasus ."

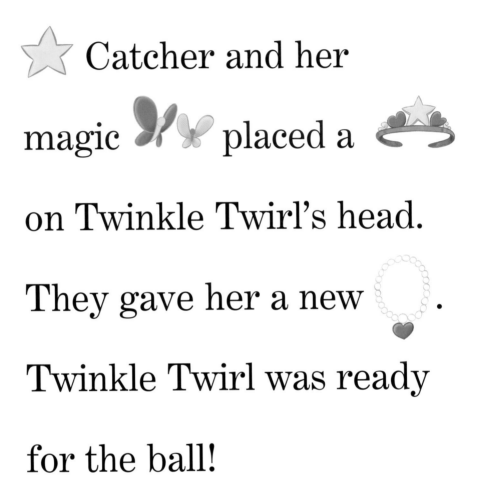 Catcher and her

magic placed a

on Twinkle Twirl's head.

They gave her a new .

Twinkle Twirl was ready

for the ball!

Twinkle Twirl went

to the .

The  were

happy to see her.

"Thank you for being

kind and helpful.

You are the best friend

ever!" they cheered.

She got a special .

Twinkle Twirl was

the ⭐ of the ball.

But the best part of all was

being with good friends–

best friends forever!

I Can Read!™

BEGINNING
1
READING

Hide-and-Seek

by Jennifer Frantz
illustrated by the Thompson Bros.
and Robin Cuddy

HARPER
An Imprint of HarperCollinsPublishers

"What a fun day

to play outside!"

said Petal Blossom.

The  was high

in the sky.

And all the

and the

were in full bloom.

"What should we do today?"

asked Sparkleworks.

"Let's fly a  !" said

Meadowbrook.

"Let's pick !"

said Star Swirl.

"I know," said Petal Blossom.

"Let's play hide-and-seek!"

"I'll be *it*," said

Meadowbrook.

She started to count,

"1 . . . 2 . . . 3 . . ."

When she got to ten,

she opened her

and said, "Ready or not,

here I come!"

Meadowbrook saw

Petal Blossom first.

Her was sticking

out from behind a 🌳 .

Meadowbrook tagged her

friend's 👃 playfully.

"I found you, Petal

Blossom!"

"I am always the first to

be found!" Petal Blossom

said, smiling.

Next, Meadowbrook saw

Sweetberry's

poking out of a .

"Gotcha, Sweetberry!"

Next, Meadowbrook looked

behind the 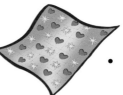 .

Then she looked behind the .

Where are my friends

hiding? she wondered.

Soon she saw Star Swirl's

 beneath a .

"You are tagged, Star Swirl,"

said Sweetberry.

But where was Sparkleworks?

"We will help you find her!"

said Star Swirl.

Sweetberry found a .

Star Swirl found a little .

Petal Blossom found a .

But none of the ponies could

find Sparkleworks.

Can you?

"Sparkleworks is the

best hider!"

Meadowbrook whispered

to the other three ponies.

"If *we* can't find her, maybe

we can make *her* find us.

Let's have a 🍵 party!"

Petal Blossom got

the .

Star Swirl gathered

pretty  in a bunch.

Sweetberry poured

make-believe .

Soon Sparkleworks heard laughter in her .

She smelled the scent of  in her .

Then Sparkleworks'  peeked out.

She saw her friends on the  having a fun  party.

50

Sparkleworks came out of

her hiding place.

"Hiding is fun," she said.

"But finding your friends

is even better!"

I Can Read!

BEGINNING
1
READING

my little Pony™

Sleepover Surprise

by Ruth Benjamin
illustrated by Josie Yee and Carlo Lo Raso

HARPER
An Imprint of HarperCollinsPublishers

Inside every 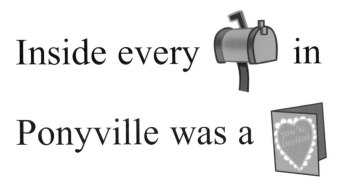 in

Ponyville was a

from Cherry Blossom.

She was having a

 party!

All of the

were invited.

The invite read:

Please come to my  party

tonight at midnight!

We will have  and  .

Bring your favorite

 to share.

Be sure to take a nap

so you are not too sleepy!

Love, Cherry Blossom

Petal Blossom was

the first  to get ready.

She loved parties!

She put ～～ in her hair.

She put on her 👕 .

She took a nap.

Triple Treat made

for the party.

She put on her  .

She took a nap.

Star Swirl picked

to bring to the party.

She tied the

with  .

She put on her  .

She took a nap.

Skywishes wished

she could take a nap.

But she was not tired.

She put on her dance

and her .

She danced until

the went down.

Back at home, Skywishes

put on her .

"I am sleepy from dancing

so much," she said.

She looked at the .

"It is almost time

for the party.

I will close my

for just a minute."

At midnight,

the went

to Cherry Blossom's .

They drank .

They ate .

They read .

"Where is Skywishes?"

they wondered.

The next morning,

Skywishes woke up.

The ☀ was shining.

The 🐦 were singing.

She looked at the 🕐 .

"Oh, no!" she cried.

"I missed the 👕 party!"

Skywishes heard a

knock at the .

It was Cherry Blossom

and the other  .

"I am sorry I missed the party,"

Skywishes told them.

"We missed you!" said

the  .

"So we brought the party to you!"

"Skywishes smiled.

"You are the best friends

a  could ask for!"

she said.

my little Pony™

A
Secret
Gift

by Ruth Benjamin

illustrated by Gayle Middleton

HARPER
An Imprint of HarperCollinsPublishers

Daisy Jo was a happy .

She loved working

in her .

She loved the smell

of her .

Most of all, she loved

doing nice things

for her  friends.

Butterscotch wanted to thank

Daisy Jo for being

such a great 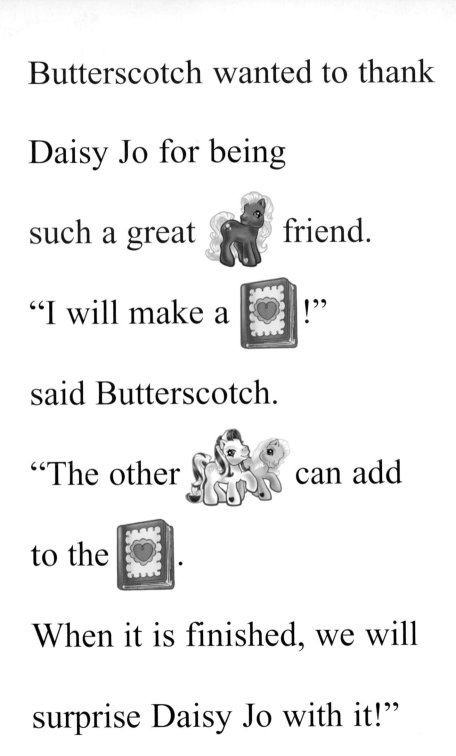 friend.

"I will make a 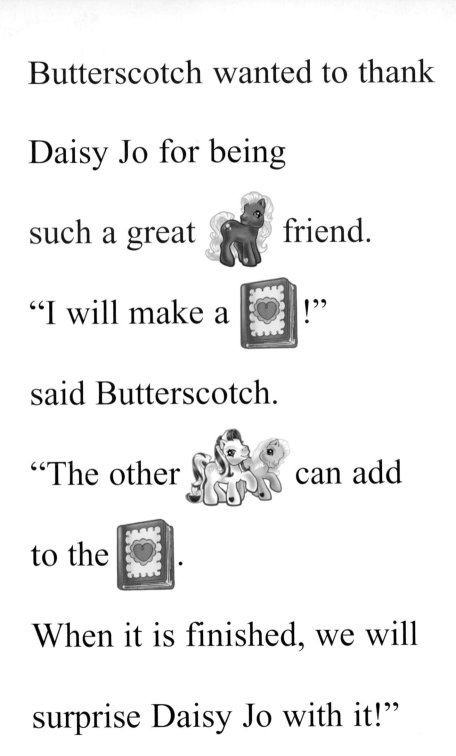 !"

said Butterscotch.

"The other 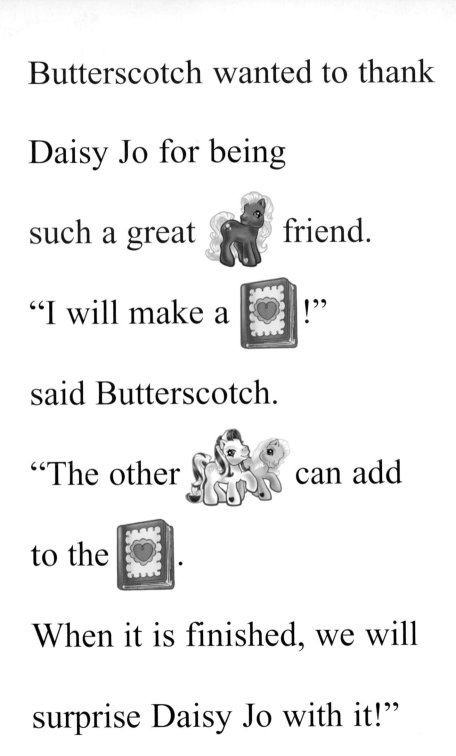 can add

to the 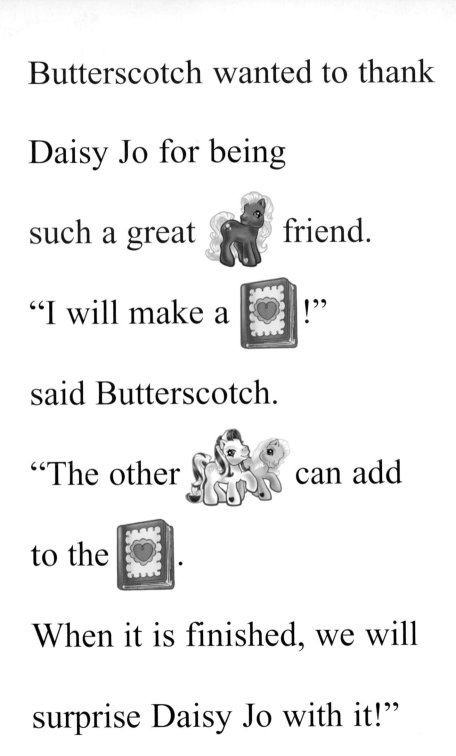 .

When it is finished, we will

surprise Daisy Jo with it!"

Butterscotch called a meeting

in the Café.

The  liked the idea!

"I will add a to the ,"

said Fluttershy.

"This of Daisy Jo

and me making a

at the beach is perfect."

"I will add dried

to the ,"

said Star Swirl.

"Daisy Jo and I both

love  .

Daisies are her favorite,

of course!"

"I will add Daisy Jo's

favorite cupcake

to the  ,"

said Sweetberry.

"Daisy Jo likes cupcakes with

 and chocolate chips.

Yummy!"

Just then, Daisy Jo walked in.

She saw the  hard at work.

"What are you doing?" she asked.

Butterscotch hid the

under the  .

"It is a surprise!" said Butterscotch.

"Meet us tonight at the Café

to find out what it is."

"A surprise," said Daisy Jo

to herself.

"My birthday is soon. . . .

Are the 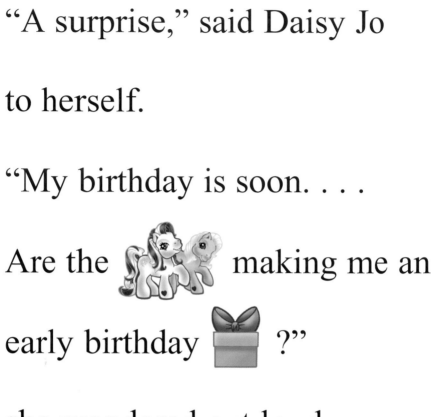 making me an

early birthday  ?"

she wondered out loud.

"What could it be?

Maybe a  ?

Or a poem?"

Back at her house,

Butterscotch looked at the .

She added a drawing

of Daisy Jo in her .

"This is filled

with good memories.

Daisy Jo will love it!"

Butterscotch said.

That night, the  met

at the Café.

When Daisy Jo walked through

the door, the  shouted,

"Surprise!"

"We made this  for you,

Daisy Jo," said Butterscotch.

"We wanted to thank you for

being such a great friend."

"Wow!" said Daisy Jo.

"I tried to guess what the

surprise would be!"

Daisy Jo was happy.

The  were the greatest

friends she could ever ask for.

"Thank *you* for being

such wonderful

friends," Daisy Jo said.

"I love my .

It is the best surprise ever!"

my little Pony™

Ponies on Ice

by Ruth Benjamin
illustrated by Carlo Lo Raso

HARPER
An Imprint of HarperCollinsPublishers

It was winter in Ponyville.

 hung from the .

The  was frozen.

The  were getting

ready for the ice-skating

party.

Each was planning

an ice dance for the party.

Triple Treat tied her  .

Then she worked on flips.

Bumbleberry tied her .

Then she worked on twirls.

Kimono put on her .

Then she tried figure eights.

Pinkie Pie watched

the other  skate.

She could not do a flip.

She could not do a twirl

or a figure eight.

What would she do

on the  ?

Triple Treat saw Pinkie

Pie sitting by the .

Pinkie Pie looked sad.

"What is wrong?"

asked Triple Treat.

"I do not know any tricks,"

said Pinkie Pie.

"I will teach you tricks!"

said Triple Treat.

"Follow me!"

Pinkie Pie tied her .

The two went out

on the ice together.

Triple Treat showed

Pinkie Pie how to spin.

She showed her

how to skate backward.

She showed her how to jump.

Pinkie Pie saw the

around Triple Treat's neck.

"This is my lucky 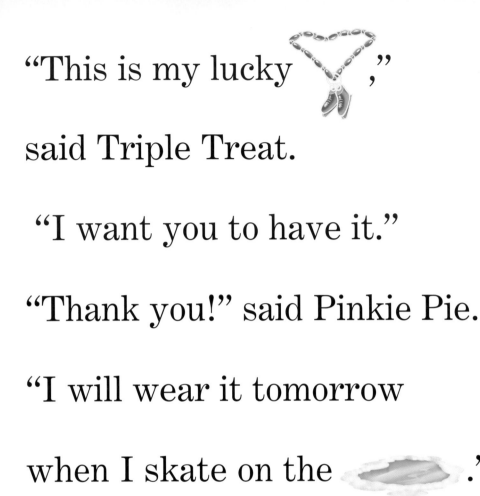,"

said Triple Treat.

"I want you to have it."

"Thank you!" said Pinkie Pie.

"I will wear it tomorrow

when I skate on the 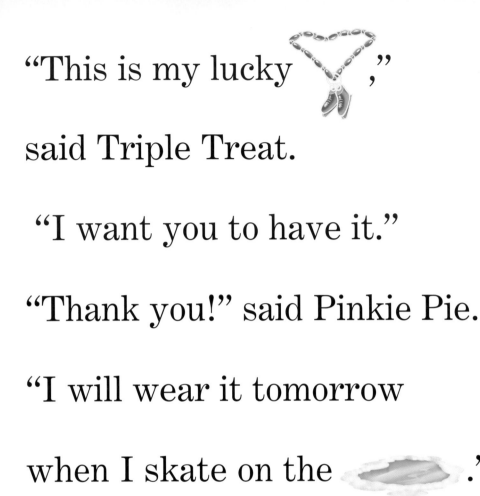."

That night as Pinkie Pie

got into ,

she thought about the party.

She wanted to show the

what she had learned.

She put the under her .

She dreamed of .

The next day, the  shone.

It was a good day to skate!

The  were dressed

in fancy costumes.

The costumes had sparkles,

, and  .

Pinkie Pie wore the  .

It was time for Triple Treat

to skate.

She asked Pinkie Pie

to join her.

They skated backward.

They did spins and jumps.

The lucky 🛼 sparkled.

"You are the star of the day!"

the  cheered.

"Thank you!" said Pinkie Pie.

And she showed them

a fun new trick.

my little Pony

Very Lucky Ponies

by Ruth Benjamin
illustrated by Lyn Fletcher

HARPER
An Imprint of HarperCollinsPublishers

It was a rainy day.

The  were dark.

Serendipity saw

something in the .

It was shiny and green.

It was a four-leaf .

She picked up the .

Suddenly the rain stopped.

The  came out.

The dark  went away.

A  sparkled

in the sky.

"Wow!" said Serendipity.

"I think this

is a lucky 🍀."

At home, Serendipity found her missing .

"I have looked all over for this !" she said.

"This  really is lucky."

Serendipity wanted to share the

with the .

She gave the

to Desert Rose.

"Now you will have

good luck, too," she said.

"Thank you," said Desert Rose.

"I will bring the

when I go to pick flowers."

Desert Rose found a field

filled with pretty .

She had never seen

 before.

"This  really is lucky,"

she said.

Then she gave the

to Scootaloo.

Scootaloo rode her

to look for 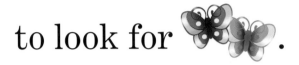 .

She saw a

with a  pattern.

She had never seen

a  before!

"This 🍀 really is lucky,"

she said.

Cupcake was baking a .

Oh, no! She ran out of .

Scootaloo came by and gave

the to Cupcake.

Cupcake checked the .

She saw a big of .

"This really is lucky,"

she said.

Cupcake wished

all the

could have a lucky .

Just as she made her wish,

a big gust of came.

The blew away.

"Oh, no!" called the .

Our lucky  is gone!"

The  looked all over

for the .

But they did not find it.

"We should not be sad,"
Desert Rose told the .
"We do not need the
to feel lucky.
We are lucky that
we have each other.
We are good friends!"

"Yes, we are!"
said the 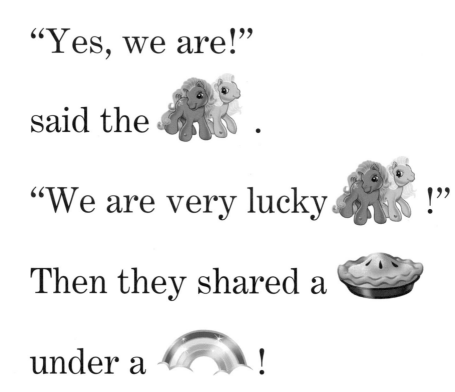 .

"We are very lucky 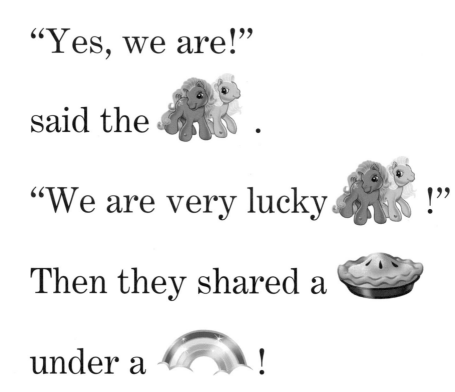 !"

Then they shared a

under a  !

Tutus and
Toe Shoes

by Ruth Benjamin
illustrated by Lyn Fletcher

HARPER
An Imprint of HarperCollinsPublishers

Twinkle Twirl's dance school

was about to open.

She had everything ready.

The  waited outside.

"Welcome to dance

school!" called Twinkle Twirl.

First, Twinkle Twirl taught
the  how to dress.
"Ballerinas wear a
and , and
in their hair.
You should pack a dance
bag with your clothes,
, and your ."

Twinkle Twirl told the

to bring  of water.

"Dancing is hard work!"

she told them.

"Spinning in your

will make you thirsty!"

Next, Twinkle Twirl taught

the 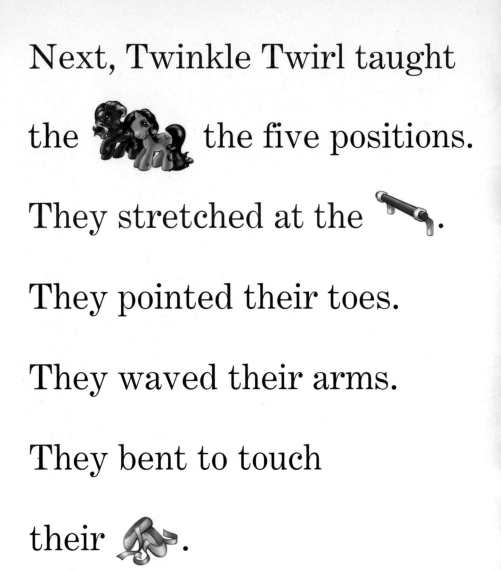 the five positions.

They stretched at the 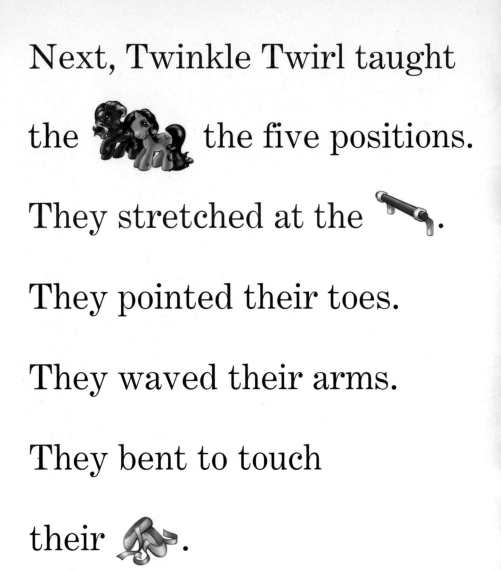.

They pointed their toes.

They waved their arms.

They bent to touch

their 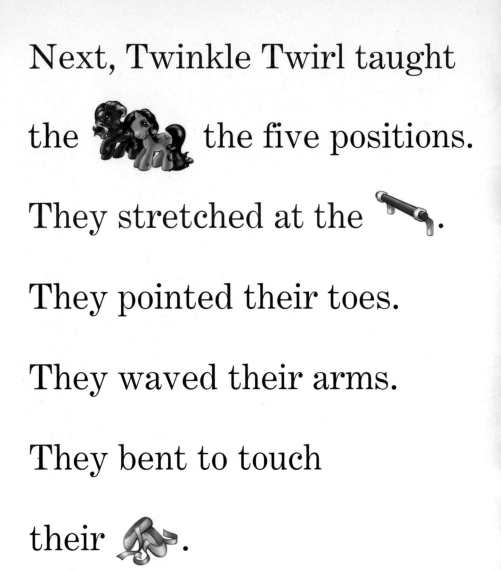.

Soon it was time

for the  to dance.

Two by two,

they moved across the floor.

They held hands

and skipped their .

Their bounced

and their twirled.

Twinkle Twirl showed the

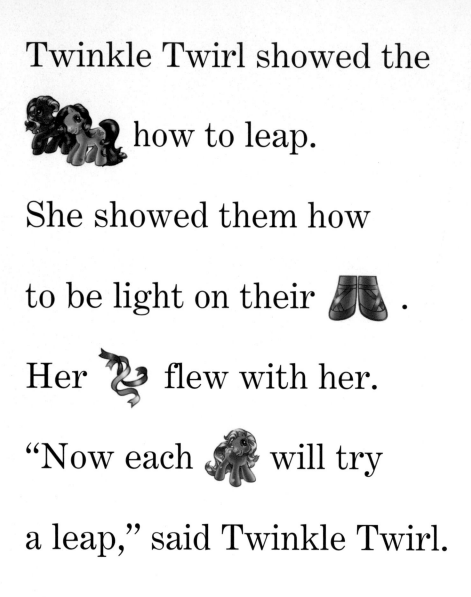 how to leap.

She showed them how

to be light on their .

Her flew with her.

"Now each will try

a leap," said Twinkle Twirl.

Pinkie Pie was afraid

to leap across the floor.

She hid behind the  .

Then she tripped

on her laces.

Oops! She fell to the floor.

"What happened?" said
Cheerilee.

"I was scared to try a leap,"
said Pinkie Pie.

"Sometimes teamwork can
help!" said Rainbow Dash.

Pinkie Pie fixed her .

She was ready to try.

The 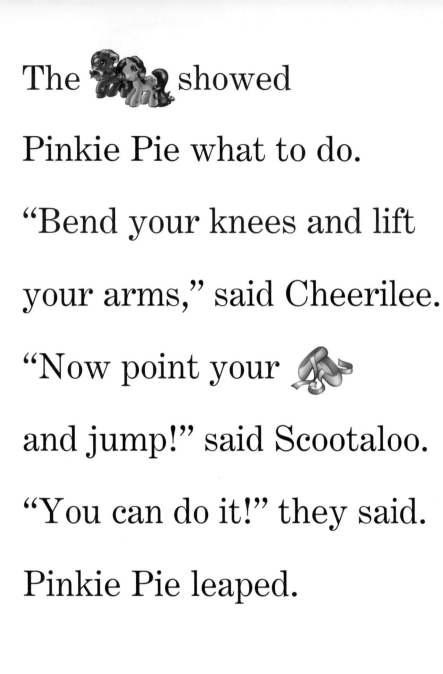 showed

Pinkie Pie what to do.

"Bend your knees and lift

your arms," said Cheerilee.

"Now point your

and jump!" said Scootaloo.

"You can do it!" they said.

Pinkie Pie leaped.

The  cheered.

"Hooray!" said Twinkle Twirl.

Rainbow Dash gave

Pinkie Pie  .

"I could not have done it

without you," said Pinkie Pie.

"Friends are the best part

of  dance school!"

Pinkie Pie took a bow.

"I can't wait to come back!"

she said.

BEGINNING 1 READING

my little Pony

Caps in the Air!

by *Karen Sherman*
illustrated by Lyn Fletcher

HARPER
An Imprint of HarperCollinsPublishers

Graduation day was here!

Rainbow Dash was very happy.

She put on her pretty .

She put on her pretty .

She shook her head.

Her twirled.

It was time to go!

The  skipped

through Ponyville.

The was shining.

The was blowing.

Their twirled.

Then Rainbow Dash said,

"My is gone!"

The  looked up.

They saw the in the air.

It flew like a kite.

The was like a tail.

The blew away.

"Oh, no!" said Rainbow Dash.

"What will I do

without my 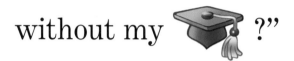 ?"

"Don't cry!"

Scootaloo said.

"We are your friends.

We will help you find it!"

First, the  looked

in the .

"Remember when I was too

shy to sing?" said StarSong.

"You made me brave!"

Rainbow Dash smiled.

But her

was not there.

Next, the  looked

on the .

"Remember when we lost

a big game?" said Scootaloo.

"You cheered me up!"

Rainbow Dash smiled.

But her was not there.

The  went to look

in Cheerilee's beauty shop.

It was closed for graduation.

"Graduation!"

said Rainbow Dash.

"We'll have to hurry.

I'll go without my  ."

CLOSED

The  ran

to the  .

They were just in time.

Rainbow Dash

went up on the stage.

She got her  .

"Well done,  !"

said Cheerilee.

"We are graduates!

We worked hard.

And we worked together.

It's time to throw

our  in the air!"

All the  cheered.

They tossed their

high in the air.

The twirled.

"Are you sad?" asked StarSong.

"We did not find your ."

"No," said Rainbow Dash.

"I am a graduate!"

Rainbow Dash said.

"I worked hard.

I do not have a .

But I do have my friends!"

Belle of the Ball

balloons

necklace

brush

ponies

butterflies

pony

cake

prize

castle

ribbons

clock

star

crown

stars

kite

wind

Hide-and-Seek

birdbath

nose

ears

quilt

eyes

rosebush

feet

shed

flowers

sun

frog

tail

grasshopper

tea

kite

tree

ladybug

trees

Sleepover Surprise

 birds

 books

 card

 clock

 cookies

 door

 eyes

 flowers

 hot chocolate

 house

 mailbox

 pajamas

 ponies

 pony

 ribbons

 shoes

 sun

 tutu

Secret Gift

 flowers

 pony

 garden

 present

 kite

 recipe

 lemons

 sand castle

 photo

 scrapbook

 ponies

table

Ponies on Ice

bed

pillow

crowns

pond

feathers

ponies

hat

pony

ice skates

scarf

icicles

sun

necklace

trees

Very Lucky Ponies

 bag

 pie

 book

 ponies

 butterflies

 rainbow

 butterfly

scooter

clouds

 sugar

 clover

sun

cupboard

sunflowers

 grass

 wind

Tutus and Toe Shoes

 barre

 bottles

 feet

 flowers

 hairbrush

 piano

 ponies

 pony

 ribbons

 toe shoes

 tutu

 tutus

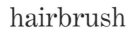
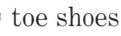

Caps in the Air

breeze

school

cap

soccer field

caps

sun

diploma

tassel

gown

tassels

ponies

theater